MUSLIM CHILDREN'S LIBRARY

A prayer at Bedtime
Author: Zaynab Dawood
Illustrators: Bookmatrix team
Cover Design: Stevan Stratford

Published by
The Islamic Foundation
Markfield Conference Centre
Ratby Lane, Markfield
Leicester LE67 9SY
United Kingdom
T (01530) 244 944
F (01530) 244 946
E i.foundation@islamic-foundation.org.uk

Quran House, PO Box 30611, Nairobi, Kenya

PMB 3193, Kano, Nigeria

British Library Cataloguing in Publication Data
    Dawood, Zaynab
        A prayer at bedtime. - (Muslim children's library)
        1. Prayer - Islam - Pictorial works - Juvenile fiction
        2. Nightmares - Pictorial works - Juvenile fiction
        3. Children's stories - Pictorial works
        I. Title II. Islamic Foundation (Great Britain)
        823.9'2 [J]
    ISBN-10: 0 86037 560 9

Printed by Proost International Book Production, Belgium

*Allahumma bi-ismika
amutu wa ahya*

O Allah in Your Name
I live and die*

*Sleep is considered as a
form of death*

A Prayer At Bedtime

by Zaynab Dawood

Dedication
I dedicate this book to my children
May Allah bless them

Abdullah is a very good boy. Everyday he plays out in his garden. And what a beautiful garden he has, *Masha'Allah*. It has tall apple trees with bright red apples hanging from their branches, and a pear tree with crunchy green pears. There are lots of plants and flowers too. His grandfather and mummy take care of the garden, wearing thick gloves and using heavy rusty spades.

There are lots of fluttering butterflies, crawling spiders, slimy snails and buzzing bees. Abdullah stays very busy in his garden, digging wriggly worms, watching leaf crunching caterpillars and feeding the birds. He has lots of fun…except for the cat. The neighbour's cat. A big, furry, green-eyed cat with long whiskers and sharp claws.

9

One day Abdullah was playing in the garden. As he bounced his ball, the cat watched him. His green eyes were fixed on the ball and his silver whiskers twitched.

Suddenly the cat jumped and went for the ball. Abdullah screamed.

"Mum!" Abdullah ran inside the house puffing and panting.

"Abdullah it's only a cat. You should be a strong boy," said his mummy. Abdullah was scared of the cat, it always watched him and ruined his games.

"I think I'll stay inside mummy," he said. So he stayed indoors for the rest of the day.

11

That night Abdullah could not get to sleep. He tossed and turned in bed. He hugged and tugged his blanket. He looked around his bedroom and saw something very strange in the corner. Amongst his toys and clothes, he could see little green eyes. He closed his eyes tightly. He did not open them. Eventually poor Abdullah fell asleep.

13

Next morning Abdullah was eager to get out of his bedroom. He went to see his grandfather.

"I had a nightmare last night about a horrible cat, a tiger with big eyes and sharp teeth and claws," he said.

"Oh dear," replied his grandfather in a soothing voice. "Maybe you should learn a *du'a* and read it before you go to sleep at night."

"But I was very scared."

"Don't worry, every time you read your *du'a* you'll become a stronger boy and not even the wildest cat will be able to scare you, *Insha'Allah*," smiled his grandfather.

Abdullah wanted to be a strong boy. So he began to learn his *du'a*. The *du'a* was very short: *Allahumma bi-ismika amutu wa ahya*. But then he heard his daddy washing the car. Abdullah ran to him.

"Daddy, please can I help?" he asked.

"Your sister is helping too," his daddy replied. As they washed the car Abdullah got very wet.

In bed Abdullah could not say his *du'a* because he did not learn it. He tossed and turned in bed, and hugged and tugged his blanket. Eventually he fell asleep.

He began to dream. It was dim, he couldn't see clearly. There was water, lots of water. Something moved in the creepy waves. It was Salma.

"Help! Help!" she cried.

Abdullah was swimming in the water too.

"Help! Help!" he shouted.

Suddenly Abdullah woke up. Very frightened and confused, he climbed out of bed and ran into his sister's bedroom.

Nudging his sister, tears fell from his eyes. Salma woke up and switched the lamp on.

"What is it?" She asked.

"I had a bad dream…about you and me…there was water…we were in danger," he sobbed.

She gave her little brother a cuddle.

"Silly, it was only a dream. Not real, look, we're here and we are both fine, thanks to Allah. Every night I say my *du'a* and that makes me feel stronger. You should listen to grandfather and learn the *du'a*. Then you won't have any nightmares and not even the most violent waves will touch you, *Insha'Allah*."

19

After breakfast Abdullah began to learn the *du'a*.

"Shall I help you?" asked grandfather.

"Yes please."

Abdullah sat on his grandfather's lap. He loved his grandfather, with his warm smile, grey beard and wrinkly hands.

"You see, Abdullah, Allah can take care of everyone. Allah wants us to be good and strong, so at night we must say our *du'as,* to make us strong," explained his grandfather.

Like a good strong boy he began to learn the *du'a*. Some words were easy and some were difficult. *Allahumma bi-ismika amutu wa ahya.*

Outside the weather changed. The sky got darker
and the wind howled, swishing all the plants around.
The neighbour's cat meowed and whimpered, and
the branches of the fruit trees tapped and scraped the
windows. Abdullah watched from the window and saw
the rain pelt down onto the ground.

"It's a storm," he thought. And what a harsh and noisy
storm it was.

23

24

With his lamp on there was a small yellow glow in his room. He tried to say his *du'a* but he could only remember a few words, *"Allahumma........ahyah."* He tossed and turned in bed, he hugged and tugged his blanket. He tried and tried, but could not remember the whole *du'a*.

His body became tired but the sound of the stormy weather kept him awake. The wind hissed and the rain whooshed. He looked towards the window. Creak, creak. The branches of the apple tree tapped his window. He was so scared that he thought he saw a creepy hand on his window, but it was only a branch with five twigs. Poor Abdullah. He leapt out of bed and ran into his parent's room.

Bright and early, Abdullah's mummy made breakfast for everyone.

"As-Salamu 'Alaikum everyone. Let's have breakfast. We all need to talk to little Abdullah," said mummy. Everyone sat around the table, including tired Abdullah.

Daddy spoke first: "Son, sometimes you are a brave boy, *Al-Hamdulillah.*"

Abdullah smiled.

"But for the past few nights you have had some scary dreams," said mummy.

Abdullah frowned.

Now grandfather spoke.

"Our brave little Abdullah. If you learn your *du'as* and read them before you sleep you won't have any bad dreams, *Insha'Allah.*"

"Have you learnt your *du'a?*" asked his sister.

"Nearly, I'm trying my best," replied Abdullah.

"*Masha'Allah,* that's good. And remember that sometimes dreams are made up of what happens to you during the day. So when the cat jumped at your ball, you had a bad dream about a wild cat. Now do you understand?" said his mother.

Abdullah smiled. He understood. He also knew that he should learn his *du'a*. During the day he learnt his *du'a*. What a happy strong boy he was.

That night he went to sleep and said his *du'a:*

"*Allahumma bi-ismika amutu wa ahya.*"

27

Feeling fresh and very brave, the next morning he
leapt out of bed. He had no bad dreams.
Al-Hamdulillah. He knew that his prayer at bedtime
helped him and that Allah will always protect him.